ARKHAMANIACS

ARKHAMANIACS

written by **Art Baltazar** and **Franco**

drawn, colored, and lettered by **Art Baltazar**

cover by **Art Baltazar**

KRISTY QUINN Senior Editor
STEVE COOK Design Director – Books
AMIE BROCKWAY-METCALF Publication Design

BOB HARRAS Senior VP – Editor-in-Chief, DC Comics
MICHELE R. WELLS VP & Executive Editor, Young Reader

JIM LEE Publisher & Chief Creative Officer
BOBBIE CHASE VP – Global Publishing Initiatives & Digital Strategy
DON FALLETTI VP – Manufacturing Operations & Workflow Management
LAWRENCE GANEM VP – Talent Services
ALISON GILL Senior VP – Manufacturing & Operations
HANK KANALZ Senior VP – Publishing Strategy & Support Services
DAN MIRON VP – Publishing Operations
NICK J. NAPOLITANO VP – Manufacturing Administration & Design
NANCY SPEARS VP – Sales
JONAH WEILAND VP – Marketing & Creative Services

Logo designed by SHAUNA PANCZYSZYN

ARKHAMANIACS

DC – a WarnerMedia Company.

DC Comics, 2900 West Alameda Ave., Burbank, CA 91505

Printed by LSC Communications, Crawfordsville, IN, USA.

10/30/20. First Printing.

ISBN: 978-1-4012-9827-2

Library of Congress Control Number: 2020918254

PEFC Certified
This product is from sustainably managed forests and controlled sources
PEFC
PEFC/29-31-337
www.pefc.org

Chapter One:

Did you ever wonder what
Bruce Wayne was like as a kid?
Before he became Batman?

Well, do we have a story for you!

Welcome to...
KRAKOOM!

Gotham City...

Walk
Walk
Splash
Sploosh

Well, here we are.
Where are we, Alfred?
We stand outside an apartment property owned and operated by Wayne Enterprises.

KRAAKOOM!
People live there?
Yes.

It looks so...
Dreary.
What are we doing here?

We're only here to pick up the mail.
Hmm.

When you're smilin'...
Woo-hoo!
Good morning, sunshine!
When you're smilin'...
Woo-hoo!
Good morning, tall buildings!
Good morning, Gotham!

Aw yeah!
There's no place like home!

Alfred...
Who is that?

HA HA HA HA HA HA HA HA HA HA HA

Hiya, Brucie!
PAT PAT

You know who I am?

Everyone knows who you are, Brucie!

Everyone?

That...
Master Bruce ...

He is the Joker.

And he lives here...

At the Arkham Apartments.
I get it!
owned by Wayne Enterprises.
That's how they know me!
Correct.

Ta-Dah!

Heya, Arky!
How you doing today?

Who's he talking to, Alfred?

I don't hear you saying anything.
C'mon.
C'mon.

He's talking to the building I'm afraid, sir.

What's the matter, Arky?
Did you get up on the wrong side of the balcony today?
TAP
TAP
DANCE
TAP

Morning, J!

Arky!

There's my house!

BUMP

You know it, bro!

Time for a tour!

Let's head inside and see what everyone is up to.

Welcome back.
Hiya, Chief!
SUPERVISOR

OSWALD

OSWALD
KNOCK
OSWALD
KNOCK
KNOCK

Hey, hey, Pengy-Poo!
Whatchu doin'?
Hello, Joker.
You're just in time.

What a delightful day for a swim with my friends.
Friends?

WHISTLE!

WALK
WALK
WADDLE
WADDLE
WALK

BOUNCE!
BOUNCE!
BOUNCE!

SPLASH!
SPLASH!
SPLASH!

What's up, buddy?
Hmm.
SNAP!
REACH
SPLOOSH!!

CLICK

FOOSH!

FFOOSHH!!

ZZHHHMM!!!

Chapter Two:

There sure are some interesting people living in these apartments. Wildlife, too.

Wonder if Bruce will come back?

WALD
VICTOR

Hmm?
VICTOR

How ya doin', Vic?
So... warm.
Needs to be colder.

Not cold enough?

Ah!
I can fix that!
ICE

ICE

SHUDDER
SHAKE
COLD

AAaahh...

Thanks, Joker.
No worries, Icepop!

That's Mr. Freeze to you.
Oh.

Well, you certainly are now!

HA! HA! HA! HA!
HA! HA!
HA! HA!

VICTOR

FLAP
FLY
CROWS
CROWS
JONATHAN
FLY
FLAP
FLAP

JONATHAN
Heya, Scarecrow!
What do ya know?
"Sigh."
Why do I even try?

Why am I called Scarecrow if I can't even scare crows?
I'm not worthy of the name.
Watch.

YAAAAH! YAAGAH!
YAAAAH!

Useless.

Hmm.

RRRGM!
RAH RAH!
HA! HA!
WWOOO!
HAHA!
YA
HOO

How did you...?

Maybe just stick to your real name...
Jonathan.

I'm not even worthy of that.
Just call me Steve.

Ha!
JONATHAN
Later, Steve!
Glad I can help.

JONATHAN
Um...yeah.

JONATHAN
FLAP
FLAP
FLAP
FLAP
FLAP
FLAP
FLAP
FLAP
FLAP

JONATHAN
Ugh.

JONATHAN
PAMELA

Sniff
Sniff

Ahem!

Back away from the flowers!
Slowly.
LA

Slowly...
I said!

Whew.
Ha?
SQUEEZE
Uhrp!
You don't have permission to smell my babies.
Now.
State your business.
Just saying good morning, young Pamela.

That's Poison Ivy to you, Joker.
Ha! Of course!

Mr. J?
Hello, Harl.

What are you doing out here in the hallway?
Oh, just hanging around.

He was smelling my flowers without permission.
Oh, that's bad.

DROP!
THUD!

Meow.
Of course!

REACH

ALL NATUR QUIC GROW PLANT FOOD

POUR
POUR

What are you doing, Joker?
I said to back away from the flower.
Just watch.

SHAKE
WIGGLE

GROW

Awww yeeeaahh.

Chapter Three:

No Brucie yet? But a cat is in trouble!

Who will save the day?!

Oh.
Hello,
Selina.
Have you seen my cat?

She's out there.

Miss Whiskers!

No worries!
I CAN fix this!

REACH
GRAB

PAINT BRUSH

PAINT FACE

PAINT
PAINT
PAINT

Go get her, Sparky!

BARK!
BARK!
BARK!

Ha!
Look at him go!
That's **not** how you get a cat out of a tree, **Joker**.
CATCH!
LICK!
Sparky's **bark** is worse than his **bite**.
Disgusting!
I need to find my cat.

Miss Whiskers?
Are you out here?

In the backyard?

Here, kitty, kitty...

SPLISH
WHH!

Don't even think about it, Croc!
Cats hate getting wet.

SPLISH

That goes for you too, Croc Junior!

WALK
WALK
WALK

SPLAT

SQUISH
SPLOOT
SQUISH

Not so fast!
BLOCK!

PUSH!
Back into the pool with you!

SPLASH!

Having a pet is a big responsibility, Croc!
SUPERVISOR GORDON
Keep an eye on your crocodile!
If I have to tell you again?
You're on report!

That goes for all of you living here!
There are rules to follow.

I've got my eyes on you.

Sweep
Sweep

I love living here!!!
Woo-Hooo!
Ha! Ha!
Ha! Ha!
Aw Yeah!

Chapter Four:

That was a ***lot*** of wildlife.
Good thing these apartments have a pool for the crocs!

Do you think Bruce is jealous of the fun they're having?

KRAKOOM!
WAYNE
Across town at
stately Wayne Manor...

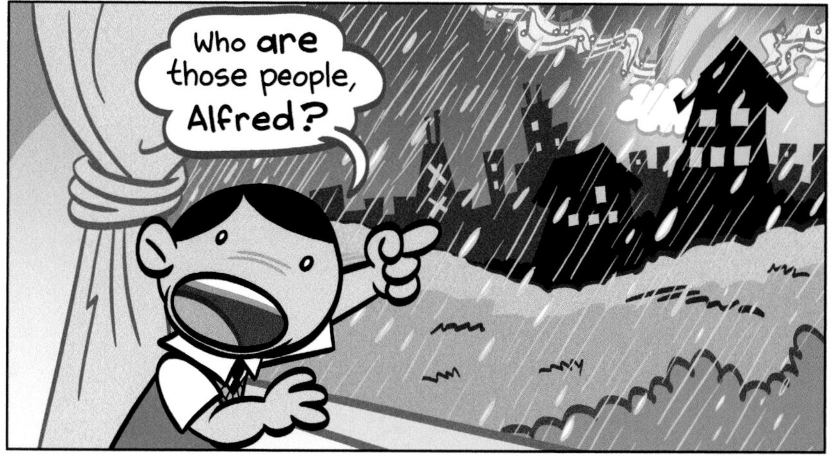
Who are those people, Alfred?

I told you, Master Bruce...
They are the residents of the Arkham Apartments.

So?

Those troublemakers don't have bedtimes.

That's great!

Come, young Master Bruce Wayne...
It's time for lunch.
And maybe a nap.

Please meet in the dining room in five minutes.
Okay.

They sure look like they're having fun.

A lot more fun than what's going on here.

Hmm.
Those Arkham people always appear to be having a great time.
They don't seem to have a care in the world.

WALK
WALK
WALK
WALK

WALK
WALK
WALK
WALK

WALK
WALK
WALK
WALK

WALK
WALK
I forgot how long it takes to get to the dining room.

WALK
WALK
WALK
WALK

Wait.
What is this room?

I don't think I've ever been in this room before.

Hello?

Gasp!

Mom?
Dad?
WAYNE

The other dining room, sir.
Oh.
Yes.
Of course.

Twenty minutes later...
I need a map to find anything in this place.
Ahem.

Late again...

Huh, son?

Where have you been, Brucie?

Sorry, Dad.
Sorry, Mom.

I went to the wrong dining room.

Again.
HOP

"Hmm."
A map is a great idea.
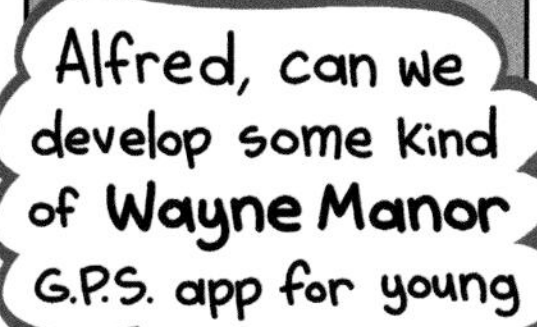
Alfred, can we develop some kind of **Wayne Manor** G.P.S. app for young Bruce?

Certainly.
I'll contact **Lucius Fox** at WayneTech right after lunch, sir.
Thank you.

How about a movie tonight, family?
The Monarch theater is playing our favorite old movie.
A classic!
Sounds wonderful.
Again?
MONARCH
Another black-and-white movie?
Can't you just stream it?

We have a giant **HD** flat-screen **TV** and **Alfred** can make popcorn!
Besides, I'd rather go out and play!

Master Bruce was introduced to the residents of the Arkham Apartments earlier today.
Oh, is that so?

Quite a colorful cast of interesting folks over there, I must say.
MONARCH

Arkham?
Why would you go over there? There's so much to do here.

Listen to your mother, Bruce.
Sounds to me like you're bored.

Alfred!
Yes, sir?
Can we get Brucie a hobby?
Like say...
A horse or a zebra or a unicorn?
MONARCH

I'll look into some options, sir.

Good.
Then that's the end of the discussion about that.
SIP

WAIT!
What just happened?

Later that night...
Time for bed, Master Bruce.
Right. Right.

I hope you enjoyed the movie, sir.
I did.

Get some Shut-eye.

Breakfast in the morning in the dining room.
Try not to get lost this time.
I'll remember, Alfred.

Okay, g'night.
CLOSE

FLIP

TIE

HAT

TOSS

CLIMB

BZZZT
BZZT

BOUNCE
JUMP
CLIMB

Chapter Five:

Sneaking out is not a great plan,
Master Bruce Wayne.
Danger awaits in the night!

GRRRR!

Oh.

GRRRR!
GRRRR!
GROWL!

YIP!
YIP!
YAP!

YAP!
YAP!

Puppy?

Ah!

Okay, okay!

Thanks, boy.
A job well done.
Some attack dog.
Beware, intruders!
You will be licked into submission!

Okay, okay.
Which one are you?
Ace!
ACE

Nice to meet you, Ace.
All right, all right!

I can't play now.
I'm on a secret mission.

We can play when I get back.
CLIMB

BOUNCE

POP!

You're just gonna follow me, aren't ya?

Okay.
C'mon, let's go!

Minutes later...
We have a special mission, Ace.

We need to find out what goes on in that place.
The Arkham Apartments.

What's the matter, boy?
Do you see something?

"Hmm..."
Something weird for sure.
We must be cautious.

I can't sleep!

I have a strange feeling, my pretties.

A feeling like we are being watched!

Hhh!!
There!
On the top floor!

Uh-oh.

I think she saw us!

ULP

Explain yourself.

Brucie?
Hey.
Welcome back.

So glad to see you in the middle of the night!
Sorry I woke you up.
Mmm.

HA! HA!
No worries!
I never sleep!
I do.

But... you're wearing pajamas.
Ha.
Yeah.
Do you like them?
Well... um...

C'mon! Let's meet everyone!

OSWALD
KNOCK KNOCK
Wake up!

VICTOR
KNOCK KNOCK
Wake up!

~~JONATHAN~~
STEVE
KNOCK KNOCK
Wake up!

HARLEY
KNOCK KNOCK
Wake up!

SELINA
KNOCK KNOCK
Wake up!

CROC
KNOCK KNOCK
Wake up!

Wha?
OSWALD

Huh?
STEVE

Who?
SELIN

SNORE!!!

Mr. J?
HARLEY

What's the meaning of this, Joker?!
Why did you wake us up?

Brucie!

This is everyone!

Everyone?

Brucie's back!

Hi, Brucie!!!

Oooh!

And is this **Alfred** with you?

Um...no, sir.
That's my puppy.

Ace.
Woof.

Of course!

How precious!

So, Brucie?
As in Bruce Wayne?
Yes.

You are kind of cute.

I may just take you to my prom one day.

AAHH!!!

Wait!
Brucie!
Leaving so soon?
?

Ha.
Oh.
He'll be back.

What happened?
I told him he was cute.

Hey!
What's with all the racket out here?
It's after hours and people are trying to sleep!

You need to break up these shenanigans before you all get written up!
ZWOOM
ZIP
ZSSHH
FFOOOM

"Heh."

Manny?
Sorry to disturb your vampire hours.

S'alright!
SLAM!

Chapter Six:

Okay, that's not the kind of danger I expected.
What a fun visit!

Do you think Bruce will be allowed
to go back if he asks politely?

WAYNE
The next morning...
DRAW
DRAW
JOKER
HARLEY
ME

ME

Is something wrong,
Master Bruce?

No.
Why do
you ask?

You seem
preoccupied.
I noticed you
gazing over at the
Arkham Apartments.

It's... it's... it's just there are
all these people over there...
And they look
and act so...
Different.
As we discussed
before, sir.
They...
I
Know!
I
Know!

They're like...
Really different.
They don't seem to care what anyone thinks about stuff.
Like... how they look.
Or how they dress.
Or how they act.

Oh, never mind.
You wouldn't understand.

Maybe you can help me understand.

I **do** have to run an errand for your father.
An errand?

Can we drive past the Arkham Apartments?

I suppose.
I'll get my shoes!

FOOSSH!

I'll meet you by the limo!

Minutes later...

What's taking Alfred so long?

FLAP
FLAP
FLAP
FLAP

Birds?

Robins.
Huh?
The birds, sir.
They are robins.

Get used to it, Master Bruce.
You should be seeing lots of them appearing here at Wayne Manor.

Lots of robins?
Wh-wh-why?

It's springtime.

PFF!

Let's go, Master Wayne.

These errands aren't going to run themselves.
Oh, right!

SWOOOSH!
SKREEK!
CHIRP!

So are we going in, Alfred?
The apartments are on the way.
We will pass by.

Can we go in?

I don't think...
Pleeaase?

Please, please?
Can we?
Can we?
Maybe.
But pay attention.
There are rules.

A very short visit is what I recommend, sir.
Easy and slow.
Take your time.
Get to know them over time.
You don't want to just **jump** right in.
JUMP!
GOOD MORNING, SUNSHINE!
THUMP!
Please remove yourself from the roof of the vehicle, you...

Oh, lighten up, Alfie.

LEAP
HOP

Did you bring him?
Bring who?

TAP
TAP

BBZZZZ

There you are!
Hiya, Brucie!
So glad you came back!

I see you brought your puppy, too!

I've got something to show you!

Mr. Joker.
Would you please give Master Bruce some space?

Ease up, Alfie.
Your boy's okay.

Mr. Joker?

Yyyeeessssss?
What did you want to show me?

Brucie!
This is your lucky day!

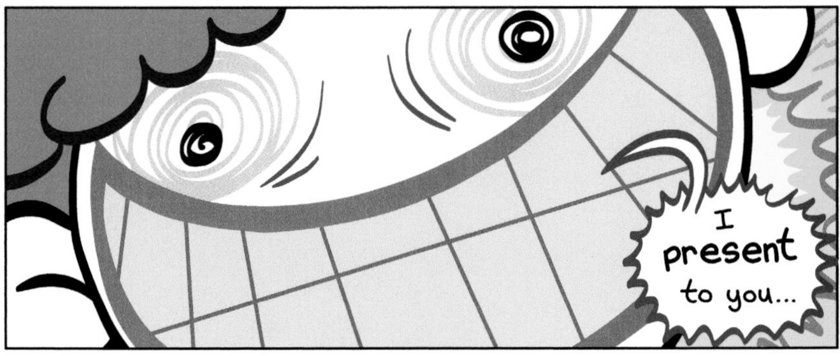

The Arkham Apartments!

Chapter Seven:

This fellow seems proud of his apartment building.
It's truly a special place to live!

I...I...
I don't...
It's just a big...
House.

What do you mean?

It's smiling right at you!

I don't see it.

You don't?

Hmm.

You just have to try harder.

Okay.
Show me.

Perfect!

Close your eyes.

Concentrate.

AH-OOOM...
AH-OOOM...

Now...
Open!

WELLLL?
How about now?
Nothing.
Still?

This is going to take a bit more effort.
Huh?
HA HA HA HA HA!

BUMP
Oh.
Heh.

Ha ha...
Supervisor Gordon.
Yeah, yeah.
I'll be right back!

Effort?
What do you suppose he means by that?
I don't try to understand the residents here.

Hello, I'm Alfred.
I know.
I'm James Gordon.
Ha.
I knew that, too.

Oh, Brucie...

Aren't you coming?

Coming where?

To our pool party, silly.

We've got penguins!
And a pool!
That's true.
We do.

Alfred?
Can I go swim?
They have penguins.

Oh, let him, Alfie!
We also have a pirate ship.
Yeah.
Come see.

LOOK!

Hi, Brucie!
Ugh.
What's he doing here?

Master Bruce...
I don't see a pirate ship.
However, we have pools at Wayne Manor.
Inside and outside.

And besides, you don't have a swim suit.

But they have penguins!

Ivy...
Will you do the honors?
"Grrumble."
I suppose.
"Mmmm."

GRAB
WHOA!
GRAB
SPIN
SPIN
Looking good, my friend.
Ready for a swim?

CANNONBALL!

Maybe we should reconsider, Master Bruce.
No way.
I want to find out what's going on.

Oh, Brucie...

Choose your weapon.

REACH

Ooh! Good one!

AH-HA!

Wait... wait...
wait... wait...
One second.

PPSSSSHHH

SQUEAK
SQUEAK

BING

EN GARDE!

Chapter Eight:

How did this happen?!

A nice visit to the Arkham Apartments,
a refreshing swim, and now a sword fight?
What other unexpected treats could today hold?

SWOOSH
SQUEAK
SQUEAK

ARRRRG!
When last we met, I beat you fair and square!
You shouldn't have come back!

Ha!
Ha! Ha! Ha!
The sharks must have found me...
Indigestible.
Good one, Captain Brucie!

Wait.
Sharks?

Did he say sharks?
Yes.
Yes, he did.

You may have survived the sharks, hero.
Let's see how you do against...
The crocodiles!

"AAHH!"

Oh, good.
Crocs.
That's much better.

SPLASH!

PLOOP!

MAN OVERBOARD!

USS Joker
TOSS

THUNK!

PLOOP!

WE HAVE A MUTINY!
BLUB

The prisoner is escaping!

Prisoner?

That's right!
He knows where the treasure is!
The pirate booty?

It's true.
We must find Captain Brucie.
But first...

LET'S HIT HIM WITH A CANNONBALL BLAST!

AAH!

PAMELA
ED

Stop right there!

Riddle me this...

My damp and drippy interloper...

The more you take...

The more you leave behind.

What are they?

Footprints?

THUMP!

Correction, Captain!

Wet footprints!

He's over here, boys!
Come get 'im!

SWOOSH!

RUN
RUN
RUN

BUMP!

Riddle me this...
My confused and bewildered compatriot.
Who or what is really, really big and blocking the hallway?

Bane!

Aahh!

Yep.
Good luck with that.

GULP.

CRACK!

Mmm...

CRACK!

TOSS

Pretzel stick?
Yeah!
PRET-
ZELZ

JUMP

Run Run

Swoosh!

Pant
Pant
Breathe

Hush.

What?

Hush.

Okay.

I'm trying to be as quiet as I can.

Hush.

Hush.

Sshh.

Nice to meet you, Sshh.

Hush?
Yes.

I gotta go.

Chapter Nine:

Bruce has made quite a few friends at the Arkham Apartments, but there's a mysterious figure around the next corner.

AAH!
Hey.

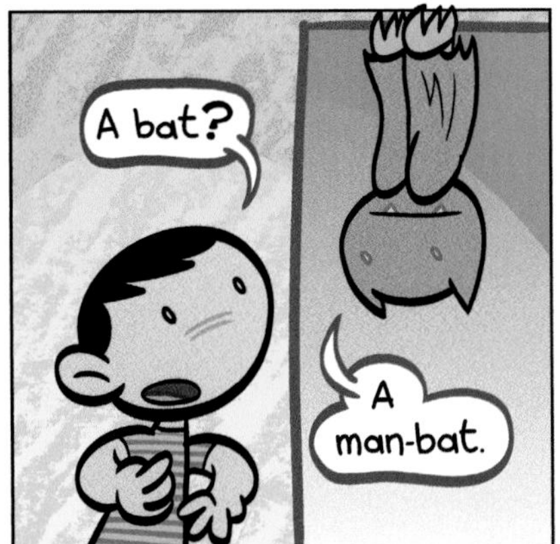
A bat?
A man-bat.

A man-bat?
Yeah.
My name is Manny.

What are you doing?
Um.
Wings?
What?
Wings.
You need wings.
I can get you wings.
Hold on.

Moments later...
Looks good!
Right?

Water wings?

Bat wings!
FLAP
FLAP
FLAP
FLAP
You're gonna need them to defeat the pirate Joker.

How do...?
I hear all.
I see all.

I am a creature of the night.
I am the terror who brings nightmares to all.

But it's daytime.

So it is!

Go see **Clayface.**
He has something for you.

Clayface?
Yeah.

He lives in the room next door.
CLAY

CLAY

Hey!
CLAY

There he is!

Get him!

SPLASH!
SPLASH!
SPLASH!

Come in.
CLAY

TURN

SPLASH!
CLAY
SPLASH

Hello?

Is anybody here?

Mr. Face?
SQUISH
SQUISH
SQUISH
SQUISH

Yuck.
What a messy room.
There's mud all over the place.

It's not mud.
It's clay.

ÄAHH!!

SLIP!

Oh.
And call me Clayface.

Wait.
You're the whole room?
"Heh."
Yep.
Not only the room...
I can take the shape of anything I want to be.

Like a puppy...

Or an elephant...

Or a couch...

Or a little Brucie Wayne.
Interesting.

Manny said you had something for me?
Yes.
Yes, I do.

I have something that will help you defeat the Joker.

I have these cool water wings.

You're gonna need more than water wings.
You're gonna need a little bit of MAJ.

Maj?
What's maj?

A little bit of iMAGination.

Now close your eyes.
Imagine those water wings working for you.
I already tried this with the Joker.
Tut-tut. Try again.
Concentrate. Use your maj.
And when you open your eyes—
Wow.

So, how long do they do this?
SPLASH
SPLASH
They can go for days.

Or until there's a winner.

Sometimes I go to bed and then wake up and they're still going.
I'm worried.
We need to find Bruce.

RUMBLE
SPLASH

I have a feeling he's about to make an appearance.
SPLASH
RUMBLE
SPLASH

CAPTAIN WAYNE...
Here to save the day!
Ha!
First Mate Clayface, too!
Ooh!
Good to see you, Brucie!
Oh, I mean...
Captain Brucie Wayne.
Cool water wings, bro.
HA HA HEE HOH!
Thanks.
Wait until you see what happens next!

Not only am I a pirate...

I'm also a **space** pirate!

BOUNCE

Not only am I a space pirate...

SPLASH

Blub
Blub

I am also a Superhero!
Oh, and by the way...
These are bat wings!
Impressive costume.
I gotta say...
Not bad for a first try.
I agree.
Nice.
Ooh.
It can use some tweaking.
Aw yeah, bat wings.
That's right.

Aw no!
I told you guys over and over!

No mud in the pool!
Um, it's clay.

Everybody out!
It's time to clean the pool!

What am I gonna do with you... you...
Say it. Say it.

Arkham people!

Ooh.
So close.

Bruce.
It's time to leave.
Okay.

Bye, Brucie!
We'll miss you!

That was fun.
We should do this again.
Oh.
We will.
Ha!

I guarantee it.

So long, Brucie!

The... the...
it... it...
smile... teeth!

My job here
is done.

Alfred! Alfred!
I saw it! The house!
It smiled at me!
Of course it did, sir.
Perhaps you will feel better after lunch.
For real!
I saw it!

—Use your MAJ.

franco aureliani

Franco Aureliani is an Eisner Award–winning writer and artist who last worked on *Superman of Smallville* for DC Books for Young Readers. Other greatest hits include the Dino-Mike book series, *Patrick the Wolf Boy*, and *Aw Yeah Comics!*, as well as critically acclaimed comics like *Superman Family Adventures*, and the *New York Times* bestselling, multi-Eisner Award–winning series *Tiny Titans* and *Super Powers* for DC Comics. He has also worked on *Grimmiss Island* and *Itty Bitty Hellboy* with Dark Horse Comics. Franco is also one of the principal owners of Aw Yeah Comics retail stores. When he is not working on comics, Franco can be found shaping young minds as a high school teacher.

art baltazar

Art Baltazar is one of the creative forces behind the *New York Times* bestselling, Eisner Award–winning DC Comics series *Tiny Titans*. He is also the co-writer of *Billy Batson and the Magic of Shazam*, *Young Justice*, and the *Green Lantern: The Animated Series* comic, and is the artist/co-writer of the awesome *Tiny Titans/Little Archie* crossover, *Superman Family Adventures*, *Super Powers*, *Superman of Smallville*, and *Itty Bitty Hellboy*. Art is one of the founders of Aw Yeah Comics comics shop, and he's also the co-creator of the ongoing comics series of the same name. He stays home and draws comics and never has to leave the house where he lives with his lovely wife, Rose, sons Sonny and Gordon, and daughter Audrey.

Have you ever wondered what's at the bottom of the sea? Why polar ice melts? Or which tools forensic scientists use to solve a crime? Well, the Flash and some of his close friends are here to take readers on a journey to answer these questions and more!

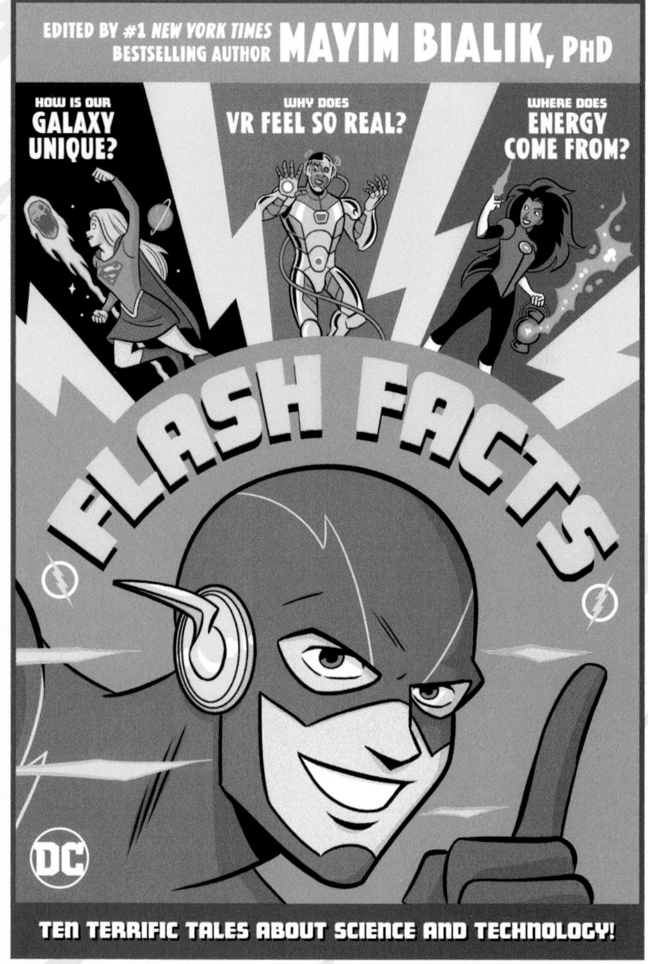

EDITED BY #1 *NEW YORK TIMES* BESTSELLING AUTHOR MAYIM BIALIK, PHD
HOW IS OUR GALAXY UNIQUE?
WHY DOES VR FEEL SO REAL?
WHERE DOES ENERGY COME FROM?
FLASH FACTS
DC
TEN TERRIFIC TALES ABOUT SCIENCE AND TECHNOLOGY!

Award-winning actress and author **Mayim Bialik**, PhD, brings together an all-star cast of writers and illustrators in this anthology, including **Michael Northrop** (*Dear Justice League*), **Cecil Castellucci** (*Batgirl*), and **Kirk Scroggs** (*The Secret Spiral of Swamp Kid*)!

Well, Supes. Looks like we finally met our match.
You may be right, my cowled companion. But if I know one thing about the two of us, it's that we never pass up a challenge.

What do you mean, good one? That wasn't funny, Cyborg.
Well, that's how this works. You know? It makes you believe your eyes, even though it's all a big trick.

Dude. Bro. Dude, bro. I don't follow.

Bro. Dude. Bro, dude. Really? 'Cause I am about ready to drop some heavy knowledge on you.

Can it wait? *Umm,* the spaghetti. The sauce. The extra cheese.
The extra cheese can wait, Beast Boy.

I cannot believe those words came out of your mouth.

I'm still me, my man. I haven't changed. I just know there are things even cooler than extra cheese.
Huh?
Like what?
Technology!
Technology?

Virtual reality!

I think your VR goggles were on too tight.

No. They fit perfectly.
But that *is* what I'm talking about. These goggles. These controllers.
The whole VR system is basically here to trick you into believing your eyes. Now do you see why it was funny?

All right, all right. Let me start from the beginning.

CLICK

You were Batman less than a minute ago. Right?

Batman on a ski lift, catching parm snowflakes on my tongue, ready to ski down Spaghetti Slopes. Yeah.

But were you *really* the Caped Crusader?

Close, but not quite.

But in VR, for a second there, you actually felt like you *were* Batman. Right?

Yeah.

VIRTUAL

And soaring over a mountain of spaghetti actually made me feel like I was hungry, too.

That's the reality part of things. You ***see*** things virtually, and they ***become*** your new reality.

VIRTUAL REALITY

CHIRP. CHIRP. CHIRP...

So what you're saying is that my head is like a video game controller.
Yes! That's it.

I bounce around, and the game sees me bounce.
I jump, it jumps. I spin, it spins.

Yes. But...
What? I knew there was a but.
STiLL MORE!

There's always a butt.

"The LED lights help with something called tracking. That's placing you in the world. But there's also something inside those goggles that is really important.

"It is called a gyroscope: three rings inside the goggles use gravity to spin around and tell the VR system how fast you're changing direction, if you're standing still, if you jump, bump, or..."

Exactamundo, my green friend.
But there's one more thing.

"In VR, we can be the size of a blue whale.
"Or the size of a leafcutter ant. It's *amazing!*"
You know who you're talking to, right?
I know, I know. But in VR, the rest of the world gets to experience how cool it is to be you!
How amazing is that?
Want to learn more about VR—
or at least see these two finish their run down Mount Spaghetti?
Check out FLASH FACTS, coming in February 2021!